WORLD OF WOW WONDER

THE AWESOME BOOK OF

DUCKBILLS AND BONEHEADS

Get ready to hear your kids say, "Wow! That's awesome!" as they dive into this fun, informative, question-answering series of books! Students—and teachers and parents—will learn things about the world around them that they never knew before!

This approach to education seeks to promote an interest in learning by answering questions kids have always wondered about. When books answer questions that kids already want to know the answers to, kids love to read those books, fostering a love for reading and learning, the true keys to lifelong education.

Colorful graphics are labeled and explained to connect with visual learners, while entertaining explanations of each subject will connect with those who prefer reading or listening as their learning style.

This educational series makes learning fun through many levels of interaction. The in-depth information combined with fantastic illustrations promote learning and retention, while question and answer boxes reinforce the subject matter to promote higher order thinking.

Teachers and parents love this series because it engages young people, sparking an interest and desire in learning. It doesn't feel like work to learn about a new subject with books this interactive and interesting.

This set of books will be an addition to your home or classroom library that everyone will enjoy. And, before you know it, you too will be saying, "Wow! That's awesome!"

"People cannot learn by having information pressed into their brains. Knowledge has to be sucked into the brain, not pushed in. First, one must create a state of mind that craves knowledge, interest, and wonder. You can teach only by creating an urge to know." - Victor Weisskopf

© 2014 Flowerpot Press

Contents under license from Aladdin Books Ltd.

Flowerpot Press
142 2nd Avenue North
Franklin, TN 37064

Flowerpot Press is a Division of Kamalu LLC, Franklin, TN, U.S.A. and Flowerpot Children's Press, Inc., Oakville, ON, Canada.

ISBN 978-1-4867-0506-1

Written by:
Michael Benton

Illustrators:
James Field
Ross Watton (SGA)
Sarah Smith
Cartoons: Jo Moore

American Edition Editor:
Johannah Gilman Paiva

Designer: Flick, Book Design & Graphics
Simon Morse

American Redesign:
Jonas Fearon Bell

Copy Editor:
Kimberly Horg

Educational Consultant:
Jim Heacock

Printed in China.

CONTENTS

INTRODUCTION

Find out for yourself all about horned dinosaurs, bonehead dinosaurs, and dinosaurs that had a bill like a duck.

Spot and count!

Dinosaurs lived on Earth millions and millions of years ago and were among the most successful animals of all time. Scientists called "paleontologists" are constantly unearthing amazing information and making exciting new discoveries about duckbilled, horned, and bonehead dinosaurs. They study their remains, called "fossils," which have been preserved in ancient rocks.

Q: Why watch out for these boxes?

A: They give answers to the dinosaur questions you always wanted to ask.

zoom in on...

Dinosaur bits
Look out for these boxes to take a closer look at dinosaur features.

Awesome facts
Watch out for these diamonds to learn more about the truly weird and wonderful facts about dinosaurs and their world.

WHEN THEY LIVED

Dinosaurs lived between 230 and 65 million years ago (mya). This is a very, very long time ago. It's hard enough to imagine hundreds of years ago, let alone millions. Dinosaurs are dated according to the geological time scale, which is used to age rocks. Geologists work out the ages of ancient rocks by studying radioactive elements in them, and by analyzing fossils.

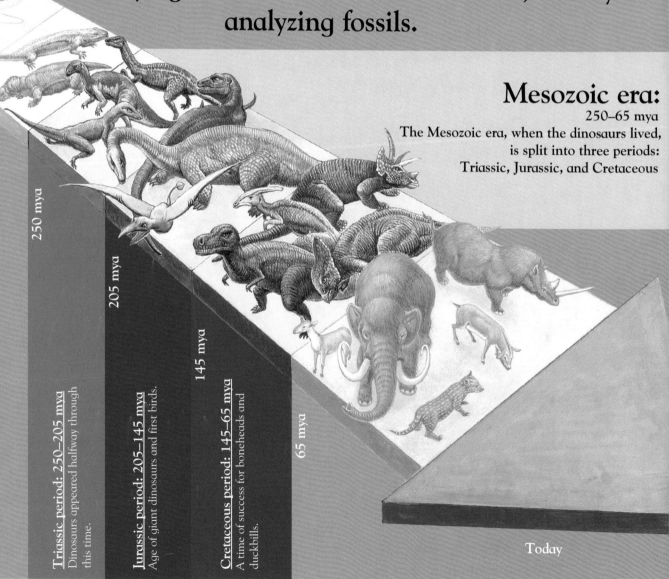

Mesozoic era:
250–65 mya
The Mesozoic era, when the dinosaurs lived, is split into three periods: Triassic, Jurassic, and Cretaceous

250 mya

205 mya

145 mya

65 mya

Triassic period: 250–205 mya
Dinosaurs appeared halfway through this time.

Jurassic period: 205–145 mya
Age of giant dinosaurs and first birds.

Cretaceous period: 145–65 mya
A time of success for boneheads and duckbills.

Today

At the start of the age of the dinosaurs, the continents were all joined together as one great supercontinent called "Pangaea." Over millions of years, the Atlantic Ocean opened up and Pangaea split apart. The continents drifted (moved slowly) to their present positions. They are still moving about an inch (a few centimeters) each year.

Today

50 mya

100 mya

200 mya

Continental drift

Pangaea

Q: How did a flesh-eating dinosaur become a fossil?

A: Small meat-eating animals ate the flesh from dead dinosaurs' bones. Some bones rotted. Others were buried under layers of sand or mud. These turned into fossils over time, as tiny spaces in the bones filled with rock. Millions of years later, the fossilized bones are uncovered by water or wind action. Paleontologists dig the fossilized bones out of the rock and clean them, making sure they don't fall apart. They make maps and take photographs at the dig site so that they can tell later exactly where everything was found.

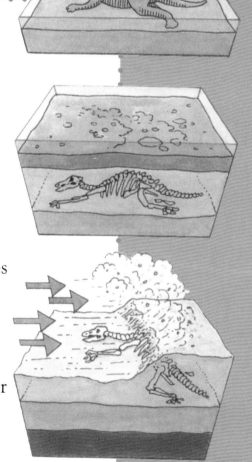

HORNS, BONES, AND BILLS

Duckbills and their relatives were part of the group of two-legged, plant-eating dinosaurs called "ornithopods." The bonehead group, called "marginocephalians," included the boneheads themselves, called "pachycephalosaurs," and the horn faces, called "ceratopsians."

Stegoceras

Duckbills and boneheads were key dinosaurs of the Cretaceous. In the Late Cretaceous of Canada, herds of the ornithopod "Lambeosaurus" lived alongside the ceratopsian "Styracosaurus" and the smaller pachycephalosaur "Stegoceras." All the duckbills and boneheads were plant eaters.

Awesome facts
Duckbills and boneheads traveled in huge mixed herds like modern antelope and wildebeest. Hundreds of skeletons have been found in some fossil beds.

Lambeosaurus

Styracosaurus

WHAT MAKES A DUCKBILL?

Duckbilled dinosaurs called "hadrosaurs" were the most successful dinosaurs of all. Hundreds of their skeletons have been found in Late Cretaceous rocks in China, North America, and Mongolia. Hadrosaurs had much the same body, but the heads were very different, often with bizarre crests.

Although hadrosaurs looked like ducks, and may have been able to swim, they spent most of their time running about on dry land. Their huge tails were used for balance. Thin rods of bone called "ossified tendons" ran along the side of the tail and over the hips. These helped to keep the tail stiff.

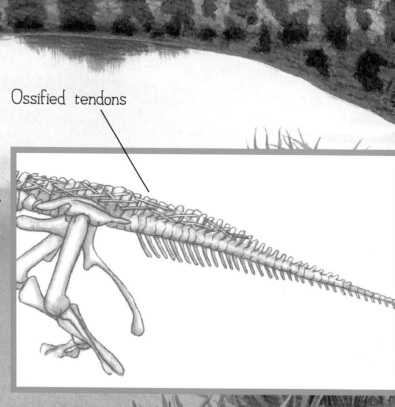

Ossified tendons

Duckbill teeth

Duckbills had hundreds of teeth arranged in tight rows, all designed for chopping tough plants. Some had as many as 2,000 teeth in total.

zoom in on...

Corythosaurus

One of the best-known duckbills, Corythosaurus of North America, had a crest shaped like half a plate on its head. It had small hooves on its fingers and toes, suggesting that it walked on all fours. However, Corythosaurus also used its hands for grabbing food.

EARLY ORNITHOPODS

The duckbills were common in the
Late Cretaceous, but the ornithopod
group had been around since the
Triassic. The early ones were small
and fast-moving, so they could
escape from predators.

Lesothosaurus

Lesothosaurus had five fingers on
its hand, just like a human, which
shows that it was a primitive form.
Most dinosaurs born later had only
three or four fingers. Lesothosaurus
used its strong little
hands to gather leaves,
and maybe even to
carry them off if it was
disturbed.

Q: What did Lesothosaurus eat?

A: Like all ornithopods, it ate plants. As it closed its jaws, its teeth rubbed firmly against each other. Its teeth could cut plant stems as if with a large pair of scissors.

Heterodontosaurus

Heterodontosaurus means "different-tooth lizard." It had long canine teeth, rather like a dog. These were not used for piercing flesh, but probably for grasping tough plant stems.

Canine teeth

LONG-DISTANCE JOURNEYS

By the Middle of the Jurassic period, duckbills and their relatives lived worldwide. One famous one, Dryosaurus, was found in North America in 1894. A similar dinosaur was discovered in Tanzania, Africa, in 1919. By 1970, it was realized that they were identical.

Middle Jurassic

North America

Atlantic Ocean opens up

Possible migration routes

Africa

Identical dinosaurs across the world means long-distance migration. The Atlantic Ocean only began to open in the Middle Jurassic. Before then, Dryosaurus could easily have hiked from America to Africa on dry land.

Plant eaters often migrated huge distances in search of food. In hot, dry climates, they might have followed the wet seasons north and south to maintain a constant supply of leaves.

How many Dryosaurus can you spot?

Dinosaur dung

How do we know what dinosaurs like Dryosaurus ate? Fossils of dung, called "coprolite," have been found with chopped up leaves and stalks in them. Like horses, dinosaurs probably couldn't digest it all, so some came out in their dung.

zoom in on...

Dryosaurus had strong arms that it used to reach leaves. Its jaws were lined with broad teeth, good for chopping up stems. But it had a special feature, seen in all the dinosaurs of the ornithopod group—a horny beak at the front of the jaws, which it used to cut and bite plants.

Dryosaurus

NAMING THE BEAST

Many skeletons of the ornithopod Iguanodon have been found in Early Cretaceous rocks in southern England, Belgium, France, and Germany. Iguanodon had a wicked thumb spike, which it may have used to defend itself.

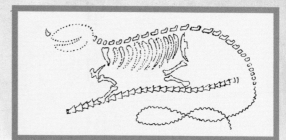

Early collectors only had a few bones of Iguanodon, and they thought a heavy, pointed bone was a nose horn (above). Only when whole skeletons were found in 1877 did they see that this bone was in fact the thumb spike.

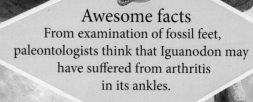

Awesome facts
From examination of fossil feet, paleontologists think that Iguanodon may have suffered from arthritis in its ankles.

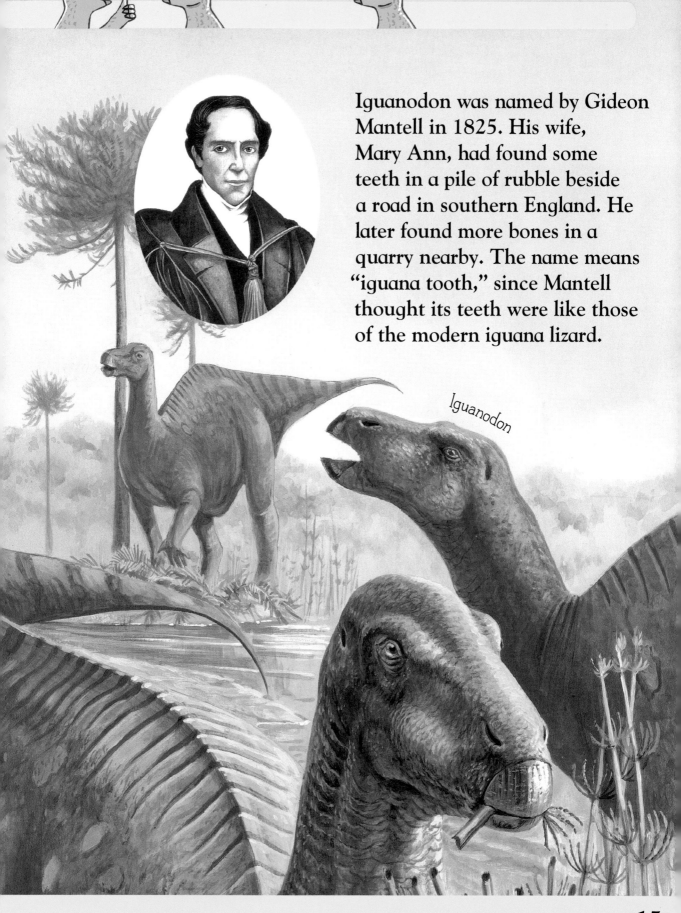

Iguanodon was named by Gideon Mantell in 1825. His wife, Mary Ann, had found some teeth in a pile of rubble beside a road in southern England. He later found more bones in a quarry nearby. The name means "iguana tooth," since Mantell thought its teeth were like those of the modern iguana lizard.

Iguanodon

RUNNERS

Hypsilophodon was a small, fast-moving ornithopod.
Great herds of them lived in southern England, and
close relatives have been found all over the world.
They were among the most successful dinosaurs
of their day.

Hypsilophodon

How many
runners
are there?

Stride length

Length of leg

Dinosaur speeds can be calculated by looking at their leg skeletons and footprints. When an animal runs faster, it takes longer strides—just like you! If you know the stride length (measured from fossil tracks) and the length of the leg, then you can work out the speed.

Awesome facts
Hypsilophodon could run at a speed of 20 miles per hour (32 km/h) or more, which is about the same speed as a racehorse.

Q: Did Hypsilophodon hide in trees?

A: Some old reconstructions show Hypsilophodon perching in a tree. This would have been impossible, however, because its feet would not have been able to grasp a branch. Hypsilophodon certainly hid from predators in bushes and found food among the trees, but it was definitely not an oversized perching bird!

CRESTS AND SNORKELS

The duckbills of the Late Cretaceous, the hadrosaurs, are famous for their amazing headgear—a huge range of crests, horns, and snorkel-like tubes. Scientists have debated what they were for. They may have marked out different species by their various shapes and sounds.

Parasaurolophus

Corythosaurus

Different crests made different noises. Each hadrosaur had its own special honk or squeak. In a herd of many different species, hadrosaurs of different types could look and listen for their mates.

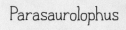

Tsintaosaurus

Males and females of a species also had different crest shapes, so they looked and sounded a bit different from each other. One of the Parasaurolophus had a shorter crest than the other, but scientists don't know whether the short-crested form was the male or the female.

Parasaurolophus had one of the most amazing crests—a long tube on top of its head. This was once thought to be a snorkel that allowed the dinosaur to breathe underwater, but there was no hole at the end. It probably allowed one Parasaurolophus to identify another.

Parasaurolophus

zoom in on...

Inside the crest

The breathing tubes in a crest ran up from the nostrils to the end of the crest, then back and down to the throat. When a hadrosaur breathed in or out, the air went all around this long set of tubes. This would have made a noise, since the tubes were like part of a trumpet.

Air

PARENTS

Amazing discoveries
have been made recently
about how duckbills
looked after their young.
Maiasaura of North
America cared for their
little hatchlings and
fed them softened plant fragments.
Maiasaura means "good mother lizard."

Awesome facts
Maiasaura hatchlings were over three feet
long before they left the nest. Until then, their
moms brought them tender shoots
and leaves to eat.

zoom in on....

Inside a dinosaur egg

Before hatching, a dinosaur
baby was very tightly coiled inside
the egg. Paleontologists have
found some dinosaur eggs
that even contain the tiny
bones of an embryo that
had died inside.

Embryo

Maiasaura mothers dug nests in the ground as big as wading pools. They laid about twenty eggs and stayed close until they hatched. They fed the babies until they were big enough to venture out alone.

 Q: Some birds nest in trees, so why didn't dinosaurs?

A: The dinosaur mom would first have had to find a strong tree, then she would have had to climb up somehow. Most dinosaurs were simply too big, or not nimble enough to manage this.

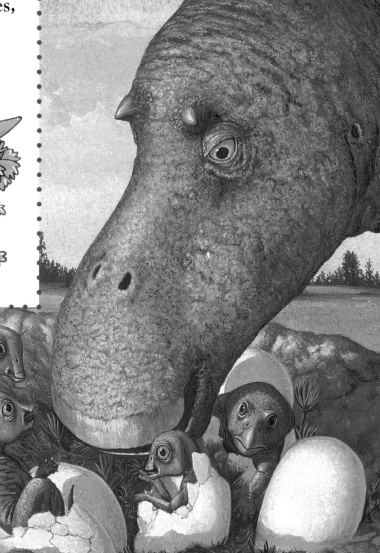

SMACKERS

The boneheads called "pachycephalosaurs" (meaning "thick-head lizards") are famous for having very thick skull roofs. The males may have had head-butting fights.

zoom in on...

Domeheads

There were two groups of pachycephalosaurs—one set with very thick, domed skull roofs, and the other with lower, flatter skull roofs.

Stegoceras

The horn faces, called "ceratopsians," probably head-butted each other. They may have sized each other up, trying to scare their rival away by appearing fierce. They roared and may even have changed the color of the bony frill around their neck. If that didn't work, they may have then crashed heads and tussled.

Just like boneheads, modern mountain goats crash heads to see who is strongest, in fights for territory or mates.

Pachycephalosaurs arose in the Early Cretaceous, but they are best known from the Late Cretaceous of North America and central Asia. They ran around on two legs, and were all plant eaters.

Styracosaurus

YOUNG AND OLD

Skeletons of baby dinosaurs show they were like human babies—big heads, big eyes, short legs, and knobby knees. One of the best series of family fossils found is of the ceratopsian Protoceratops, from the Late Cretaceous.

Awesome facts
The first Mongolian dinosaurs were named in the 1920s, when expeditions set off into remote northern regions Now, many amazing dinosaurs are known from there.

An amazing set of fossil tracks from North America shows how a herd protected its young. The tiny footprints of the babies are in the middle, with the bigger moms' and dads' footprints on the outside.

Fossil specimens from Mongolia include dozens of skulls of whole families of Protoceratops. Of course, the dinosaur became bigger as it grew older, but the shape of the skull also changed. The babies had huge eyes, short beaks, and weak jaws.

Baby

Adult

Juvenile

An amazing fossil specimen, found in Mongolia in the 1960s, shows a Protoceratops and a Velociraptor locked in mortal combat. They were killed by a sandstorm.

How many babies are there?

Protoceratops

Protoceratops

FAMILY PROTECTION

Sometimes there is safety in numbers. Similar to musk oxen today, ceratopsians may have formed a ring with their horned heads outward when a meat eater threatened. Many plant eaters could use the herd as a way to protect themselves.

Einiosaurus

Albertosaurus

Styracosaurus

Even on their own, the ceratopsians were able to look after themselves. Albertosaurus had to be careful when it was faced by the long nose horn and spiky frill of Styracosaurus.

Einiosaurus babies would stay in the middle of the group when the herd was under attack. The adults would present a united front, with their impressive horns facing the predator.

Ceratopsians had all kinds of face horns, some on the nose, others over the eyes. The neck frill also varied in size and decoration.

Triceratops

Chasmosaurus

Pentaceratops

Q: How fast could a horn face run?

A: Ceratopsians were built to move quite fast. It's likely they could trot, and even get up to twelve miles (19 km) per hour. They weighed about five tons (4.5 t)—the same as a modern elephant—and could move much faster than the giant plant-eating dinosaurs.

DUCKBILL AND BONEHEAD WORLD

Ornithopods peaked in the Cretaceous, from Iguanodon to the later duckbills. The boneheads (pachycephalosaurs) and horned ceratopsians are only really known from the Late Cretaceous.

Dryosaurus

Which ornithopod had long canine teeth like a dog?

Can you remember which duckbill had long canine teeth like a dog?

250 mya
(Million years ago)

TRIASSIC

205 mya

JURASSIC

Which two ornithopods on these pages lived millions of years before the rest?

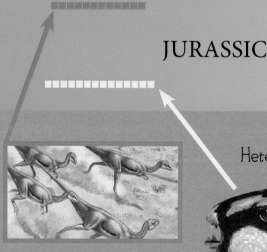

Lesothosaurus

Heterodontosaurus

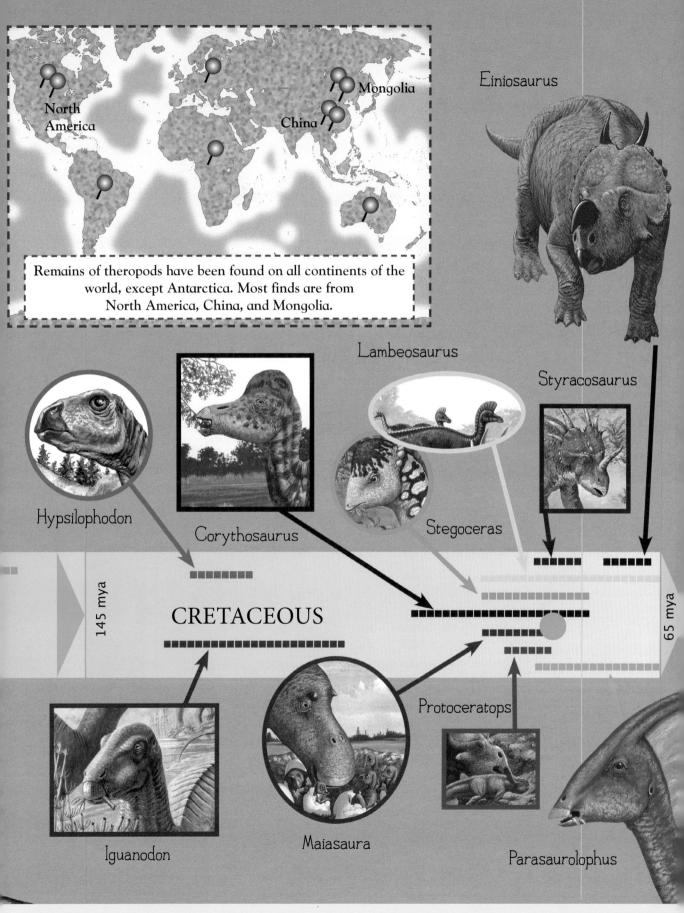

Remains of theropods have been found on all continents of the world, except Antarctica. Most finds are from North America, China, and Mongolia.

North America

Mongolia

China

Einiosaurus

Lambeosaurus

Styracosaurus

Hypsilophodon

Corythosaurus

Stegoceras

145 mya

CRETACEOUS

65 mya

Protoceratops

Iguanodon

Maiasaura

Parasaurolophus

SAURISCHIA

THEROPODA

SAUROPODOMORPHA

THYREOPHORA

ORNITHISCHIA

MARGINOCEPHALIA

ORNITHOPODA

DINOSAUR GROUPS

There were five main groups of dinosaurs: two-legged plant eaters (such as duckbills) called "ornithopods;" bonehead and horned dinosaurs, called "marginocephalians;" armored plant eaters, called "thyreophorans;" meat eaters, called "theropods;" and big, long-necked plant eaters, called "sauropodomorphs."

Corythosaurus

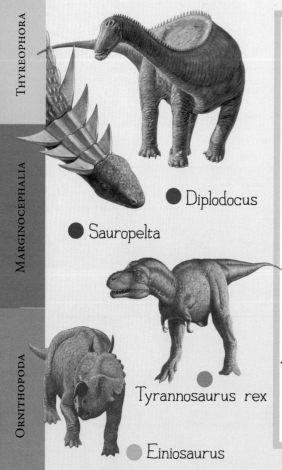

Diplodocus

Sauropelta

Tyrannosaurus rex

Einiosaurus

All dinosaurs are classed into one of two sub-groups, the Saurischia and the Ornithischia, according to the arrangement of their three hip bones. The Saurischia, or "lizard hips," had the three hip bones, all pointing in different directions. The Ornithischia, or "bird hips," had both of the lower hip bones running backwards.

Hypsilophodon (Ornithischia)

Carnotaurus (Saurischia)

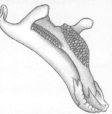

GLOSSARY

Amphibian
A backboned animal that lives both in water and on land, such as a frog.

Ceratopsian
A plant-eating dinosaur with a bony frill at the back of its neck and horns on its face.

Continental drift
The movement of the continents over time.

Coprolite
Fossilized feces.

Cretaceous
The geological period that lasted from 145 to 65 million years ago.

Duckbill
An ornithopod dinosaur of the late Cretaceous, with a duck-like snout. Duckbills are sometimes called "hadrosaurs."

Fossil
The remains of any ancient plant or animal, usually preserved in rock.

Geological
To do with the study of rocks.

Hadrosaur
Another name for a duckbill.

Jurassic
The geological period that lasted from 205 to 145 million years ago.

Marginocephalian
A plant-eating dinosaur with armored margins (borders) on its skull, like a ceratopsian or a pachycephalosaur.

Mesozoic
The geological era that lasted from 250 to 65 million years ago— the "age of dinosaurs."

Ornithopod
A two-legged plant eater from the ornithischian group, such as a duckbill.

Pachycephalosaur
A plant-eating dinosaur with a hugely thickened skull roof.

Paleontologist
A person who studies fossils.

Predator
A meat eater—an animal that hunts others for food.

Radioactive
Describes an element that gives off sub-atomic particles at a fixed rate. Measuring radioactive elements in ancient rocks helps geologists calculate the age of the rocks.

Radioactivity
The process by which an element gives up sub-atomic particles at a fixed rate.

Reptile
A backboned animal with scales, such as a dinosaur or a lizard. Most reptiles lay eggs and live on land.

Species
One particular kind of plant or animal, such as Iguanodon, the panda, or human beings.

Triassic
The geological period that lasted from 250 to 205 million years ago.

INDEX

Albertosaurus 26
amphibians 4, 31

babies 20, 21, 24, 25, 27
beak 13, 24
birds 4, 21
boneheads 6, 7, 22, 23, 28
bones 5, 6, 14, 15, 20, 30

Carnotaurus 30
ceratopsians 6, 22, 23, 26, 27, 28
Chasmosaurus 27
continental drift 5, 31
coprolites 13, 31
Corythosaurus 9, 18, 29, 30
crest 8, 9, 18, 19
Cretaceous 4, 6, 7, 8, 10, 14, 18, 23, 24, 29, 31

Dryosaurus 12, 13, 28
duckbills 6, 7, 8, 9, 10, 12, 18, 20, 28, 30, 31

eggs 20, 21, 31
Einiosaurus 26, 27, 29, 30
elephant 27

feet 4, 14, 17, 20
fingers 9, 10
footprints 17, 24
fossils 3, 4, 5, 7, 13, 14, 17, 24, 25, 31
frills 22, 23, 26, 27, 31

geological 4, 31

hadrosaurs 8, 18, 31
hands 9, 10

hatchlings 20
head 8, 9, 19, 22, 23, 24, 26
Heterodontosaurus 11, 28
hips 8, 30
hooves 9
horns 6, 18, 27, 31
horses 13, 17
Hypsilophodon 16, 17, 29, 30

Iguanodon 14, 15, 28, 29, 31

jaws 11, 13, 24
Jurassic 4, 12, 28, 31
juveniles 24

Lambeosaurus 7, 29
legs 17, 23, 24
Lesothosaurus 10, 11, 28
lizards 11, 12, 15, 20, 22, 31

Maiasaura 20, 21, 29
Mantell, Gideon 15
Mantell, Mary Ann 15
marginocephalians 6, 30, 31
meat eaters 26, 30, 31
Mesozoic 4, 31
migration 12

nests 20, 21

Ornithischia 30, 31
ornithopods 6, 7, 10, 11, 13, 14, 16, 28, 30, 31
ossified tendons 8

pachycephalosaurs 6, 7, 22, 23, 28, 31
paleontologists 3, 5, 14, 20, 31

Pangaea 5
Parasaurolophus 18, 19, 29
Pentaceratops 27
plant eaters 7, 12, 23, 26, 30, 31
predators 10, 17, 27, 31
Protoceratops 24, 25, 29

radioactivity 4, 31
reptiles 31
rocks 3, 4, 5, 14, 31

Saurischia 30
Sauropelta 30
sauropodomorphs 30
skeleton 7, 8, 14, 17, 24
skull 22, 24, 31
species 18, 31
spikes 14
Stegoceras 6, 7, 22, 29
Styracosaurus 7, 23, 26, 29
supercontinent 5

tail 8
teeth 9, 11, 13, 15, 28
theropods 29, 30
thyreophorans 30
toes 9
Torosaurus 26
Triassic 4, 10, 28, 31
Triceratops 27
Tsintaosaurus 18
Tyrannosaurus rex 30

Velociraptor 25